# Pickle *and* Lily

Annie Stewart lives in Gloucestershire with her
husband, Philip and two cats, Milly and Pickle
(who is helping her to write more stories).
She hopes to have a Welsh terrier puppy
of her own one day.

*Previous books*

Wilf Trilogy
The Adventures of Wilf (2010)
Wilf Runs Away (2012)
Wilf in Love (2016)

*For Penny*

# Pickle
## *and*
# Lily

*Happy Reading!*

Annie Stewart

*Annie Stewart*

The Book Guild Ltd

*16/9/2019.*

First published in Great Britain in 2019 by
The Book Guild Ltd
9 Priory Business Park
Wistow Road, Kibworth
Leicestershire, LE8 0RX
Freephone: 0800 999 2982
www.bookguild.co.uk
Email: info@bookguild.co.uk
Twitter: @bookguild

Typeset in Century Schoolbook

Printed and bound by CPI Group (UK) Ltd, Croydon, CR0 4YY


ISBN 978 1912881 321


British Library Cataloguing in Publication Data.
A catalogue record for this book is available from the British Library.

*For Mum*

# PICKLE PURRKINS
## *and the* PICCALILLI

Pickle Purrkins sprawled lazily on his favourite windowsill basking in the early autumn sunshine and warming his black and white fur. The day stretched out before him enticingly like an undulating piece of string. He thought he might call on some of his friends and go for a walk on the beach. Saltsea, where he lived with his owners, the Purrkins family, was a pretty town right beside the sea. He could take Gertie, the chocolate Labrador, Oscar, the border terrier and Marmalade, the ginger tomcat.

He stretched and purred with anticipation and ran downstairs for some breakfast. Patsy and Peter Purrkins were finishing their morning coffee.

"I must finish making that batch of piccalilli today," Patsy said.

"Yes, and we must get things ready for Lily," Peter replied. "I wonder how Pickle will get on with her!"

Pickle, who was busy crunching biscuits, pricked up his ears. *Lily? Who was Lily?*

"Well, we will soon find out!" laughed Patsy. Later that morning, on his way out of the cat flap, Pickle spied a jar of

yellow mixture on the kitchen shelf with a label on which said
PICCALILLI. Oh, so that was it, Pickle thought. Of course,
Piccalilli; that's what they meant by Lily. It must be a treat
for his tea. It wasn't a very nice colour but perhaps it tasted
nice with biscuits.

It was a crisp, sunny morning and Pickle had a brilliant
time on the beach with Gertie, Oscar and Marmalade. They
all paddled and chased waves and then collapsed on the
warm, soft sand. Marmalade didn't really like getting wet so
he started cleaning his damp fur.

"Has anyone heard of piccalilli?" Pickle asked.

"No," chorused Oscar and Marmalade.

"Well…" said Gertie slowly, "my human, Michael, makes chutney – is piccalilli yellow?"

"Yes!" said Pickle. "It looks really horrible!"

"It doesn't look as if it tastes very nice," Gertie agreed. "Best to try it and see, then if you don't like it, you'll know for next time."

Pickle decided this was good advice. He said goodbye to his friends and set off for home. Time for some lunch. As he let himself in through the cat flap, he could hear voices and laughter. Peter and Patsy Purrkins were in the kitchen and Ben and Molly, their two children, were kneeling on the floor talking to something. What was it?

As Pickle got nearer, Molly squealed in delight. "Oh, it's Pickle, come and meet Lily!" Pickle peeped nervously over Molly's shoulder. A pair of bright brown eyes met his gaze. The owner was an energetic ball of brown and black fur that whimpered and bounced up and down with excitement on seeing Pickle. Lily was not the strange yellow mixture in the jar. Lily was a dog!

The first thing Pickle noticed about living with Lily was that he didn't get any attention any more. Ben and Molly were always with Lily and poor Pickle couldn't help feeling left out and a bit jealous. His friends were understanding and tried to cheer him up but it didn't help...

One afternoon on the way back from the beach he bumped into two of his neighbours, Winnie, the bulldog and Percy, the pug.

"What's up, Pickle?" asked Winnie.

"Yes, what's the matter, Pickle?" Percy joined in. "You look a bit down in the dumps."

Pickle sighed. "Oh, it's just that my family have bought a puppy. Her name is Lily and now they don't seem to have any time for me. I don't know what to do..." Pickle flopped down on the coarse grass between the sand dunes, his head on his paws. His whiskers quivered as tears trickled slowly down his shiny black nose. Winnie and Percy sat down beside him.

"Don't get upset, Pickle," Winnie said kindly. "We felt the same when our humans bought two kittens."

"They drove us mad!" added Percy. "Swinging from lampshades, hanging off the curtains, scratching the carpets. They were always in trouble and we made ourselves scarce most of the time. We just went home for tea."

Winnie smiled. "But, after a while they grew up and now, we all get on quite well. We have great fun chasing each other. Give it time, Pickle, you might get to like Lily after a while."

"Thank you," sniffed Pickle. "I'll try my best but I'm not sure if that will ever happen!"

Pickle wearily made his way home up Cat and Mouse Lane. As he jumped through the cat flap the house seemed to be in uproar. Patsy Purrkins' sewing basket was upside down in the middle of the sitting room and there were rolls of cotton and balls of wool everywhere. He went into the kitchen where his bowl of biscuits had been knocked over, the contents scattered everywhere. He had a drink from his water bowl and decided to retreat to his basket which also seemed to have travelled to the other side of the room.

The kitchen door burst open and Lily flung herself into the room.

"Lily! Wait!" cried Molly Purrkins, on the other end of a long lead and very out of breath. The rest of the family followed.

"Goodness, I'm exhausted!" Patsy Purrkins gasped.

"So am I," yawned Peter Purrkins. "I didn't know that a puppy could be such hard work!"

"Ben, you and Molly go and finish your homework while I clear up and get dinner ready," Patsy said.

The children ran upstairs followed by the animated ball of fluff that was Lily.

Pickle stretched his paws and ventured into the sitting room where Peter Purrkins was having a quiet cup of tea. Pickle jumped on his lap.

"Miaow!"

"Oh, Pickle, poor boy, are you feeling a bit neglected?"

"Miaow!" Pickle agreed.

"Come on, let's get your dinner." Peter Purrkins went back into the kitchen where Lily, having got bored upstairs, was rolling around on one of the shelves in the pantry. "Lily, get down from there!" yelled Mr Purrkins. "You'll break something!"

# CRASH!

Too late... Six jars of the strange yellow liquid fell to the floor and smashed into little pieces. As the river of lumpy liquid travelled towards the kitchen door Patsy Purrkins rushed in. "Oh no, not my piccalilli! Lily, you naughty dog!"

Lily was banished to her basket for the rest of the day in disgrace. Later that evening Pickle heard her whimpering. He crept up to her basket and pushed his nose into her soft fur. She jumped up straight away and ran round him in circles, her tail wagging furiously. Pickle pushed her gently towards her dinner bowl and she gobbled up all her food in a flash. Then she staggered back to her basket and fell asleep, full and happy, snoring gently. Pickle sighed and went back to his own basket. She was only a baby, he thought. Winston and Percy were right, he would just have to get used to having her around.

The next morning dawned bright and sunny. After Peter Purrkins had left for work and Ben and Molly had gone to school, Pickle curled up on the landing windowsill for a nap. Patsy Purrkins was busy cooking in the kitchen singing along to the radio and Pickle felt warm and dozy. He must have dropped off because when he woke up Patsy was peering over him and Lily was curled up next to him fast asleep. "Oh, just look at you two!" she laughed. "Friends at last! Pickle and Lily, just like my piccalilli, meant to be together." Pickle purred sleepily; maybe living with a dog wasn't going to be so bad after all.

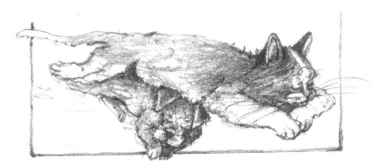

8

# PICKLE AND LILY
# MEET THE PARTRIDGES

"Well I never!" exclaimed Patsy Purrkins.

"What, dear?" said her husband, Peter, absently, immersed in the sports section of *The Telegraph*.

"How brilliant!" continued Patsy.

"Darling, whatever is it? How can I concentrate when you keep talking?" grumbled Peter.

"Well!" said Patsy, her face lit up with excitement. "It says here in the local paper that the butcher's shop in the high street is going to re-open after twenty years! Apparently, it was a butcher's originally but no one has ever made a go of it since." Peter peered over her shoulder to look at the double-page spread in the *Saltsea Star*.

"That is good news!" he agreed. "Just what the village needs."

"Yes," said Patsy. "It will be lovely just to walk down the road and buy a decent joint."

They were interrupted by the thud of the letter box and the shrill barking of Lily, their new Welsh terrier puppy. Ben and Molly Purrkins bounded down the stairs after her.

"Lily, stop that row!" shouted Ben. "I've got to go and do my paper round and it's Molly's turn to take you out." Molly sleepily retrieved the post and Lily bounded into the kitchen after her, tail wagging furiously. Pickle, the Purrkins' black and white cat, stretched his paws and sighed. He would wait until Lily had gone for her walk and have his breakfast in peace. He was still struggling to get used to living with a dog.

Breakfast over, Patsy Purrkins started clearing the dishes. "Peter, will you mow the lawn while I wash up and make a shopping list," she called.

"Okay, dear," Peter sighed, reluctantly putting down the paper. "It's Saturday and sunny; we could have a barbecue later."

"Oh, that's a great idea!" said Patsy. "Won't it be nice when we don't have to go into Saltdean to buy meat?" Saltdean was the bustling market town eight miles from Saltsea where the Purrkins family did most of their shopping.

Pickle, having finished his breakfast, decided to head for the beach. It was a lovely day and he happily rolled around in the warm, soft sand of the dunes as he watched his friends, Gertie, the chocolate Labrador and Oscar, the border terrier, enjoying their morning swim. Around midday he decided to head for home and some lunch. As he sauntered up Cat and Mouse Lane he spotted a big removals van parked on the grass verge outside 'The Roost', the farmhouse next door. He crept through the undergrowth and climbed up a tree overlooking the garden. A small ruddy-faced man was directing men with furniture and a little round woman was throwing sticks for two big dogs. Curled up on the terrace was a very large tabby cat with a torn ear. Pickle had seen enough. Time for his lunch.

The Purrkins family were all in the garden getting ready for the barbecue.

"Hello, Pickle," said Molly. "Just in time; we've invited our new neighbours round for lunch and, guess what, they're the new butchers and they've got two dogs and a cat and..."

Pickle had heard enough and was just about to disappear through the cat flap when he heard Patsy Purrkins say, "Molly, where's Lily? I haven't seen her since she came back from her walk."

Lily was not in her basket or anywhere to be seen. Barbecue forgotten, the Purrkins family started searching and calling, "Lily, Lily, come on, good girl." Pickle carried on with his lunch. *I knew it*, he thought, *a dog can only mean one thing, trouble!*

Ben called from outside in the lane. "Hey! I've just seen Mrs Chattergood from the village shop. She saw Lily outside the house about half an hour ago."

"Oh Lily, we've lost her, we've lost her!" wailed Molly starting to cry. They were just going to start searching the field opposite the house when the ruddy-faced man and the little round woman Pickle had seen earlier appeared.

"Hello!" said the man. "My name is Roly Partridge and this is my wife, Ruby. Thank you for asking us round. Have you lost something?"

"Yes, our puppy, Lily. You haven't seen her, have you?" said a flustered Peter Purrkins.

"Well, I think our dogs might have adopted her," smiled Ruby.

The Purrkins family followed Ruby into her garden with Pickle in close pursuit. There, on the patio, was Lily curled up asleep between the Partridges' two Airedale terriers, Betty and Olive.

"Betty and Olive are sisters," Ruby explained, "and they have really taken to your little Lily. I think they are mothering her."

"How sweet!" cried Molly.

Ben laughed. "I don't think your cat has taken to our Pickle though." Everyone turned round. Pickle was perched on the top of a large wicker chair hissing at the big tabby cat with the torn ear who was sprawled on the cushion.

"Oh dear," said Ruby. "That's our cat, Rufus. I think that friendship just might take a little bit longer!"

The Partridges and the Purrkins had a wonderful barbecue and the following Monday Patsy Purrkins, closely followed by Mrs Chattergood, was the first in the queue as Partridges' Family Butchers threw open its doors for the first time. Roly and Ruby were resplendent in striped aprons and straw boaters. That evening they invited the Purrkins family round for a steak supper to celebrate the opening. Pickle stayed at home sulking in his basket. He would do battle with Rufus tomorrow. Lily might have made friends with their new neighbours but she was just a puppy with a lot to learn. Cats were a little bit choosier.

# PICKLE AND LILY
# ALL AT SEA

Pickle had had a very trying week. Lily, the Purrkins family's new Welsh terrier puppy kept getting out, mainly next door to see Betty and Olive, the two Airedale terriers who lived there with their owners, Roly and Ruby Partridge, who ran the new butcher's shop. Pickle also had to contend with Rufus, their large tabby cat, who would position himself each morning in the tree outside Pickle's favourite window. Pickle liked to have a nap on the windowsill after breakfast but now he could feel Rufus's slanting amber eyes fixed on him, taunting him, until he felt duty-bound to chase him out of the garden. This morning had been no different. It was Sunday and after breakfast he retreated to his basket to plan his day. Lily had been for her walk and was snoring gently in her basket.

"I think I'll put a new lock on the garden gate, darling, and perhaps some wire netting," Peter Purrkins announced at breakfast. "That might stop Lily getting into next door's garden. We saw Betty and Olive on our walk and she nearly pulled me over trying to follow them home."

"That's a good idea," Patsy Purrkins agreed. "She so loves

those dogs but it must be annoying for Ruby and Roly. She rolled all over their vegetable patch yesterday."

Pickle was woken from his morning snooze by loud banging as Peter Purrkins worked on the gate. That was the last straw so he headed for the beach. Marmalade, the ginger tomcat, was curled up on the warm sand in the dunes with Winston, the bulldog and Percy, the pug. Gertie, the chocolate Labrador, was on the beach with her owner, Michael, enjoying her swim. Michael was talking to a couple with a young yellow Labrador who was frantically running around in circles in the sand.

"Who is that mad dog?" Pickle asked.

"Oh, that's Fizzy," Winston replied. "She belongs to Carolyn and Patrick Thompson. They are friends of Gertie's human."

"Yes, they are renting Dune Cottage from Mrs Chattergood who runs the village shop," Percy added. "They come over every morning in their little rowing boat to give the dogs a swim. Fizzy is quite young and drives Gertie mad."

"I know the feeling!" sighed Pickle.

Marmalade, the ginger tomcat stirred and stretched. "Goodness," he purred drowsily, "isn't that Lily on the beach, Pickle?" Pickle couldn't believe his eyes. Lily, bored with no one to play with, had followed him to the beach and had found a new friend in Fizzy.

"Lily!" yelled Pickle. "You stupid dog, come here!" As the animals watched helplessly Fizzy and Lily frolicked in the waves and Fizzy jumped in the rowing boat. Lily thought this was a great game and followed suit. The little boat started rocking violently. Suddenly, the rope tethering it snapped and Fizzy and Lily, still wrapped up in their game, were transported by the waves swiftly out to sea...

Everybody started shouting at once. Carolyn Thompson was waving her arms around and calling desperately, "Fizzy, Fizzy darling, come back!" Pickle hated the water but he knew he had to do something. He raced down to the beach and screamed at Gertie.

"You can swim; help me!" Gertie didn't need telling twice. She jumped into the sea with Pickle on her back hanging on to her collar. The little boat was quite far out now and Pickle could hear Lily whining. "It's okay, Lily, we're coming!" he called, in what he hoped was a comforting tone. They were almost at the boat and Fizzy started jumping up and down with excitement. The boat started rocking again and capsized, a large wave pitching the two dogs into the water.

"Oh no, now we're in the soup," groaned Gertie.

"Come on, Fizzy, swim!" shouted Pickle. "Lily, try and get on Fizzy's back like me."

The dogs suddenly became aware of a loud chugging sound. Michael, Gertie's human, had alerted his friend Colin, the coastguard. The boat drew alongside the dogs and ropes were thrown. One by one the three dogs and Pickle were pulled to safety.

Back on the beach there was quite a welcoming party including a very worried Purrkins family and their neighbours, the Partridges. "Oh Lily, thank goodness you're safe!" cried Molly as she wrapped a rug around the shivering puppy and buried her face in her damp fur.

"Fizzy, you naughty dog!" scolded the Thompsons trying to look cross but feeling very relieved that their beloved pet was back on dry land.

"Well done, Gertie, my girl!" smiled Michael. "You and Pickle kept your heads when the rest of us were losing ours."

"Yes," agreed Peter Purrkins. "Thanks to you two Fizzy and Lily are none the worse for their adventure all at sea."

# PICKLE AND LILY
# LOST AND FOUND

Pickle stretched wearily. He had just chased Rufus, the big tabby cat from next door, out of the garden for the third time and stopped Lily, the Welsh terrier puppy, from chewing the washing. Exhausted, Lily was now asleep in the laundry basket. So far, Peter Purrkins' plan to put wire netting over the gate had worked and stopped her from getting into the neighbours' garden, but that meant she just got into more mischief at home, not helped by the fact that Betty and Olive, the Airedale terriers who lived next door and loved Lily, always had their heads over the fence in the hope of seeing her. Having a puppy was certainly very hard work, Pickle decided.

As he poked his head through the cat flap in search of some biscuits the front door banged. Molly Purrkins was home from school.

"Mum, Mum, Mum!" she called. "Can we look after Georgie's rabbit this weekend?"

"Slow down, Molly. Maybe..." said Patsy Purrkins cautiously from the kitchen where she was chopping vegetables for dinner.

23

"Georgie has to go and see her grandma in London. She's not very well, and there's no one to look after Skipper. That's their bunny and he's so cute. Can we, Mum? Can we, please?"

"Oh, okay, Molly, I'm sure we can manage," sighed Patsy. It couldn't be a more chaotic household than it already was, could it? Pickle, who had been listening while he finished his tea, couldn't believe his ears. How on earth was he going to cope with a rabbit as well as Lily?

Ten minutes later Peter Purrkins arrived home.

"Hi darling, I'm starving. What's for dinner?"

"Vegetable lasagne," Patsy Purrkins replied. "Ben walked Lily so we can have it soon and Molly—"

"Oh, and by the way," interrupted Peter Purrkins, "my dad rang today. He's been invited on a golf weekend so I said we would look after Bruce for him." Bruce was Mr Purrkins' boxer dog.

"You did what...!?" spluttered Patsy.

"Well, I said we weren't doing anything this weekend," continued Peter, "and one more won't make any difference."

"It will, actually," said Patsy, "because we will have two more. Molly has promised her friend, Georgie, that we will look after her rabbit for the weekend."

"We can't look after a rabbit as well as another dog, Patsy, what are you thinking! Molly will just have to ring her friend and say no."

"Peter, she can't, she's already said to Georgie that we will do it and her grandmother is ill so they must go."

"Oh well, that's just fine, isn't it!" snapped Peter Purrkins. "I'm taking Lily for another walk before tea." Pickle, still listening, and now in his basket, was horrified. Bruce, the boxer, was grumpy and would certainly not get on with Lily let alone a rabbit. A fine weekend this was going to be!

Saturday morning arrived and the Purrkins family braced themselves for their visitors. Paul Purrkins arrived first. "Hello everyone, thanks for having Bruce, I'm sure he will have a great time. Lovely weather for golf!" he said happily and with a cheerful wave climbed back into his MG, hood down and golf clubs on the back seat. As he disappeared down the drive in a cloud of dust, a battered old Volvo estate drew up outside. Geraldine and Gordon Dobbs got out first, followed by Georgie. Molly rushed out, her face flushed with excitement.

"Good morning, Patsy," said Geraldine. "Thank you so much for doing this. The hospital says my mum is doing well so she should be home on Monday."

"Yes, here's Skipper," said Gordon. "I'll collect him Monday morning. Just need to get his hutch out of the car."

Patsy Purrkins had sat down rather suddenly. She was so shocked her legs had given way. Skipper **was** a rabbit, but an extremely large one, who apparently had his own hutch as big as a dog kennel and lived outside. Peter Purrkins came in from the garden looking very red-faced and none too pleased. "It's bedlam out there!" he moaned. "Pickle and Lily are both chasing Skipper, and Bruce has gone in the rabbit hutch to hide from next door's tabby, Rufus, who is perched on the top."

"Well, it's no good complaining now, Peter, we're stuck with this till Monday. We'll just have to cope," sighed Patsy faintly.

The family enjoyed a barbecue in the garden as it was a fine evening and eventually the animals all settled down in the right places, exhausted. Lily and Pickle were flopped in their baskets and Bruce the Boxer had been coaxed out of the rabbit hutch with a bone. He was now asleep on his tartan rug in the living room. Rufus, the tabby cat, had finally got bored and gone home and Skipper had retired to his hutch.

"Isn't Skipper lovely, Mum!" Molly gushed on her way to bed.

"Well, yes, he is, darling, I just didn't realize he was going to be so big," Patsy replied.

"Yes, but he is gorgeous, isn't he, Mum?" Molly continued. "He's an Agouti Flemish Giant and Georgie says that is the largest breed of rabbit in the world, they can weigh 7-8 kg, that's 15-18 lbs, and..."

"Okay, okay, Molly, bed now, even Flemish Giants have to sleep!"

The Purrkins family retired to bed exhausted. Ben got up early Sunday morning to do his paper round and, as Patsy was fumbling sleepily round the kitchen making coffee, he burst through the back door. "Mum, Mum, I just went to get my bike and open the gate and all the wire netting has been chewed off. Skipper isn't in his hutch and Lily isn't in her basket!"

"Oh no!" groaned Patsy. "Your father is not going to be pleased! Don't worry, they've probably only gone next door. You get off and I'll go and see Ruby when I've finished my coffee."

Patsy knocked next door at 'The Roost' and was greeted by Ruby Partridge in her dressing gown, curlers in her hair. Her husband, Roly, was just taking Betty and Olive, the two Airedales, for their walk.

"Hello, love," said Ruby. "Fancy a cuppa?"

"Hello, Ruby, I'm sorry to bother you but have you seen Lily this morning, or perhaps a large rabbit...?" Patsy faltered.

"I'm afraid not, love. Lily usually comes a bit later but that wire seems to be keeping her out which is good for our beans; a rabbit won't be though. Come and have that cuppa, love, you've gone as white as a sheet."

"Thank you, Ruby, but I really should get back," gasped Patsy suddenly feeling rather sick.

When Patsy got home her husband was storming round the kitchen in his pyjamas, eyes blazing. "Patsy, have you seen the back gate. The netting is ruined. I spent a whole morning doing that!"

"I know, Peter, but more importantly Skipper and Lily are missing and they're not next door."

Once the family were all up, they started searching. All day they searched; Ben went out on his bike and Mr Purrkins in the car. Pickle went to the beach and alerted all his friends but no luck. They called off the search at 10 pm having picked at a Sunday roast that no one felt like eating.

"What's Georgie going to say when she hears we've lost Skipper!" cried Molly.

"We should have known better," Peter Purrkins said. "What were we thinking having a puppy? Lily has been nothing but trouble since she arrived!" Pickle agreed but she was only a baby who loved everyone. What was wrong with him?! He actually felt worried about her!

The Purrkins family spent a restless night. Ben got up early again to do his paper round and Patsy decided to keep both the children off school until the animals were found. Peter Purrkins took the day off to work from home and was out walking Bruce, the boxer, when the Dobbs family turned up to collect Skipper. They were, of course, very upset when they heard what had happened and Georgie couldn't stop crying.

"I want my Skippy! I want my bunny back!"

"Don't worry, darling, I'm sure he'll turn up," Geraldine Dobbs said soothingly. "Poor Molly has lost Lily too."

They were just deciding to continue the search when Ben rushed in.

"Ben, you're very late, the papers don't usually take you this long," scolded Patsy Purrkins.

"Never mind that, Mum!" gasped Ben. "Mrs Chattergood at the shop said to me this morning that she had seen a rabbit in her garden and it was so big she thought it might be a hare. I went outside and Skipper was hopping about in the bushes. Mrs Chattergood has managed to lure him into her shed with a carrot. There's no sign of Lily though."

Everyone piled into the Dobbs' Volvo. At the shop Gordon Dobbs got Skipper's cage out and headed for the shed to retrieve the runaway. The rest of the party scoured the garden.

"Lily, Lily, where are you!"

"Here she is!" called Ben. Lily was curled up on a heap of grass cuttings at the end of the garden next to the chicken coop.

"Oh, little pet," cooed Mrs Chattergood. "I think she must have been interested in my chickens and gone to sleep, bless her." Molly picked Lily up and she opened one eye sleepily and wagged her tail.

"Come on, mischief, it's home for you," she said. Everyone got back in the car, tired but relieved. Even Pickle was pleased that Lily was back safe and sound and laid by her basket, head on paws, on guard while she slept off her adventure.

The Dobbs family stayed for lunch and then amidst many apologies and thanks all round, packed the hutch in the car and headed for home, their beloved rabbit still asleep in his cage.

"Thank goodness for that," sighed Mr Purrkins. "I'm off to fix the gate!"

No one had the energy to be cross with Lily and she looked positively angelic, asleep in her basket. "Pickle, I do believe you've missed Lily," smiled Patsy Purrkins as she put down his tea. Pickle tried to look cross but instead got on with the serious business of eating after which he intended to chase Rufus out of the garden. That tabby had got away with sitting in the tree teasing him all weekend; enough was enough!

A loud tooting of horns and screeching of brakes heralded the return of Paul Purrkins from his golf trip.

"Thanks so much for looking after Bruce for me, Patsy," he said. "I hope he's behaved himself." Bruce was ecstatic to see his master and jumped straight into the back of the car. He couldn't wait to escape the madness of the Purrkins household. "I've had such a great time!" Paul continued. "I lost a few balls but I found a few too."

"Well done, Paul," laughed Patsy and as she waved goodbye, she felt very grateful that dear Lily and Skipper had been lost and found too.

# PICKLE
## *and the* POORLY PAW

Pickle yawned and turned over sleepily in his basket. Sunlight dappled the walls and brightly coloured rug in the conservatory. It was autumn half term so he knew that the Purrkins family would be slow to rise this morning. Pickle crept cautiously into the kitchen. There was nobody about and Lily, the family's Welsh terrier puppy was snoring gently in her basket surrounded by toys and for some reason Patsy Purrkins' peg bag. Oh dear, thought Pickle, Lily did like to chew those pegs. He brushed them into a pile and headed upstairs for the landing window. Half term or not, that big tabby cat from the farm next door was going to need sorting out. Pickle peeped out of the curtains and sure enough there was Rufus sitting in the tree as usual staring at him with his big, slanting amber eyes. No time to waste thought Pickle as he ran down the stairs and out of the cat flap. That cat needed dealing with before breakfast.

On hearing Pickle's approach Rufus streaked down the tree and headed off down the path. There was a hole in the fence at the end just big enough for him to squeeze through to his own garden. Pickle was right on his tail, closer than he had ever

33

been before. Just as Rufus thought he had lost the chase there
was a loud "Miaow!" behind him. Pickle had forgotten the big
tree root at the end of the garden, all that remained of an old
apple tree, and gone flying. Rufus couldn't believe his luck and
without a second glance shot through the fence to the safety of
his own garden. His owner, Roly Partridge, the local butcher,
was busy raking up leaves.

"Hello, old boy," he laughed. "What's all that rumpus about? Is that Pickle chasing you again?" Rufus slunk into the house and Roly peeped round the fence to see Pickle on his back mewing in pain. "Oh dear, Pickle boy," he said. "Looks like you're in a bit of bother." Without more ado Roly clambered over the fence and picked Pickle up in his arms. His right front paw was badly torn and bleeding. "Come on, boy," Roly said kindly. "Let's get you home."

Patsy Purrkins was pottering drowsily round the kitchen making coffee and thinking how lovely it was to have half term and more peaceful mornings when there was a loud hammering on the back door.

"Hello, Roly, you're an early bird," she said.

"Yes, sorry, Patsy, but your Pickle has had a bit of an accident chasing our Rufus, I'm afraid," said Roly putting Pickle down on his blanket.

"Oh dear, Pickle, what have you done!" cried Patsy. "Thank you so much for rescuing him, Roly. I'll ring the vet straight away." By now Molly and Ben Purrkins had heard all the commotion and were sleepily comforting Pickle in their pyjamas. Lily had also woken up and was trying to snuggle up to Pickle, sniffing him and whining. Goodness, thought Patsy as she rang the vet, it was only Monday and already it was chaos!

Half an hour later Patsy Purrkins was in the vet's consulting room. "Well," said Wendy Wagtail, "the good news is that Pickle hasn't broken anything but now I have cleaned the wound I can see he has a nasty tear in his paw which will need stitches. I'll bandage it and he will have to rest for a few weeks. Leave him with us and we'll call you when you can pick him up."

"Thank you so much, Wendy, see you later," sighed Patsy. When she got home there was a battered old van parked in the drive. "Oh no," she groaned. She had forgotten that Peter Purrkins' best friend Andrew had come round to start replacing the floorboards in the spare room.

"Morning, Patsy," said Andrew cheerfully as he greeted her at the front door, a pile of wood over his shoulder and Lily at his heels. "I'll clear the old floor today and start laying the new one tomorrow if that's okay with you."

"That's fine," murmured Patsy faintly as she shooed Lily back into the kitchen. Today was turning into a nightmare. After a strong coffee she felt a bit better and looked at the calendar to remind herself just what was supposed to be happening this week.

"Hi Mum," said Ben Purrkins now dressed and dropping a large rucksack on the kitchen floor. "I'm all packed for Scout camp and Scott's dad is picking me up in ten minutes so I'll see you Friday."

"Okay, dear," said Patsy who had only just realized that Ben was going today. "Where's Molly?"

"Oh, she's gone off to netball club. Georgie's mum picked her up half an hour ago and they are having lunch afterwards."

"Okay, that's fine," said Patsy still trying to get a grip on the day's events. After she had waved Ben off and Andrew had finished clearing the spare room and departed until the next day Patsy had some lunch and decided to take Lily for her walk before Molly came home and she had to pick up Pickle. It felt wonderful to walk along the beach with Lily racing in and out of the waves and taking in great lungfuls of fresh, bracing air clearing her foggy brain.

As she and Lily turned into Cat and Mouse Lane, she saw Geraldine Dobbs' battered old Volvo turning into the drive. Patsy put Lily on her lead and hurried to meet them. "Hi Geraldine, Georgie, thanks for having Molly... Where is Molly?"

"I'm here, Mum," said Molly slowly getting out of the car. She had a large bandage round her left ankle and looked rather pale.

"Oh Molly, don't tell me you've fallen over too!" cried Patsy.

"I'm afraid she had a tumble at netball," Geraldine explained. "We've had it checked out at the hospital and luckily it's just a bad sprain. We went back home for something to eat as we were all starving and I didn't want to worry you when Molly told me about Pickle's mishap."

"Goodness, what a morning, Geraldine. Come and have a quick cuppa. I've got to collect Pickle at five." Molly and Georgie went upstairs to watch television with a plate of biscuits and Lily in hot pursuit. About an hour later when she had said goodbye to Geraldine and Georgie, Patsy called upstairs. "Molly, I'm just going to pick Pickle up from the vet's. Will you be okay?"

"I'm fine, Mum, just tired. You go and don't worry, Lily is up here with me asleep on the bed."

When Patsy got to the vet's Pickle was already in his cat carrier looking groggy, a large bandage on his paw. "Come on, boy, let's get you home, shall we? Molly can't wait to see you and she's hurt her leg too."

Once home Pickle limped to his basket. Ouch, his paw really hurt when he tried to stand on it. Never mind; a good sleep and a hearty breakfast would put him right, then he would sort out this annoying bandage… Pickle was woken by growling and a tugging sensation. It was Lily pulling at his bandage. Well, for once that was a good idea. Pickle grabbed the other end and between them they tried to pull the bandage off.

"Lily! Cut that out!" It was Peter Purrkins up bright and early to take Lily out and make breakfast for Patsy and Molly who were both exhausted after the previous day's events. "Pickle, you should know better. You've had stitches in your paw and that bandage is there for a reason. You need to rest," scolded Peter. Pickle felt really fed up and put his head on his paws. Rufus was going to have a fine old time with him out of action. Lily had a lovely walk and was delighted to see Andrew as they came back up the drive unloading the new wood for the spare room.

"Hi Peter, just going to get started, should be finished by tonight."

"That's great, Andrew, I'm just off to work," said Peter letting Lily off her lead. "Patsy will make you some coffee in a minute." Andrew headed upstairs whistling Lily on his heels. Lily loved the smell of the spare room; all that dust and interesting holes to explore. She wriggled into a small space and had a good old sniff around. She was feeling a bit tired now after all that fun with Pickle's bandage and a long walk. She yawned and five minutes later was fast asleep…

It was lunchtime before Patsy Purrkins realized that she hadn't seen Lily the whole morning. Andrew had finished laying the floorboards in the spare room and was coming back next week to varnish them. Between making him coffee and helping Molly with her half-term homework she had been too

busy to notice Lily's absence. What a nuisance! She must have sneaked off next door to visit Betty and Olive, the neighbours' Airedale terriers. It was time for her walk and she was due to take Pickle back to the vet's for a check-up at three. Patsy ran next door but there was no car in the drive and she knew that Ruby and Roly often took the dogs for a run in their lunch hour. "Oh well," sighed Patsy, it would have to be the vet's first and Lily later. Pickle wasn't too happy about being bundled into his carrier but his mood improved when the vet took his bandage off.

"Well!" said Wendy Wagtail happily. "I'm pleased to say that Pickle's paw is beautifully clean and has healed well. I'll just pop his stitches out and he is good to go. Keep him in for a couple of days as a precaution and bring him back if you are worried about anything but otherwise, he's fine." Pickle couldn't wait to get back home; two days and then freedom. Rufus had better watch out!

As Patsy turned into her drive, she saw Roly getting Betty and Olive out of his car.

"Hi Roly," she called having quickly put Pickle back in the house. "I'll just come round and get Lily, she's late for her walk."

"Hello Patsy," said Roly looking puzzled. "I'm sure we haven't seen Lily at all today."

"Oh dear," said Patsy turning pale. "Oh no, wherever has she got to then?"

"Now, don't panic, my dear," said Roly kindly. "I'm sure she'll turn up. I'll just get the girls in and I'll come round and help you look for her."

"Thanks Roly," sniffed Patsy suddenly feeling tearful.

"Mum, Mum!" It was Molly Purrkins standing at the front door holding Pickle. "I can hear strange noises coming from upstairs." Patsy, Molly and Pickle followed the whimpering sounds into the spare room. Pickle sniffed at the floorboards and started scrabbling furiously.

"Pickle, careful, you'll hurt your paw again!" yelled Patsy.

"Oh Mum, it's Lily," cried Molly, her eyes wide with fright. "She's got under the floorboards; she's stuck!" Lily most certainly was stuck. She had woken up from a lovely sleep to find herself in the dark and, now, no matter how she tried she couldn't find a way out. She felt stiff and hungry and frightened. She could hear voices now and started whimpering and scratching so they would hear her.

"Oh no!" said Patsy. "Andrew must have put the floorboards down not realizing that our curious Lily had decided to explore."

By this time Roly had arrived. "Well, the little tinker," he laughed. "Don't worry, Patsy, I'll go and get my tools and we'll have her out of there in a jiffy." Sure enough, Roly only had to lever up a couple of floorboards to be able to free a very distressed puppy.

"Oh Lily, you silly girlie," cried Molly tearfully, cuddling a shaking Lily. "Let's get you warmed up and have some tea."

An hour or so later Patsy waved a fond farewell to Roly who had stayed for tea and cake. Lily had eaten a huge tea and was now curled up in her basket with Pickle close by keeping watch. She really was a silly dog, he thought, but he couldn't help feeling sorry for her and she clearly needed looking after, so until he could resume guard duties, he would be her protector. By the time Peter Purrkins got home from work Patsy was exhausted.

"I thought half term was going to be so lovely and relaxing," she wailed.

"Never mind, darling," said Peter soothingly. "Andrew is coming back in the morning to replace those two floorboards and Pickle isn't letting Lily out of his sight so don't worry. Now, you go and relax and I'll go and get fish and chips. I think we all deserve a half-term treat!"

"Marvellous!" said Patsy wearily sinking onto the sofa.

By the weekend, life in the Purrkins family had returned to some sort of normality. Ben was home from a great time at Scout camp and Molly's ankle was much better. As for Lily, she was very subdued after her adventure and had been as good as gold. Pickle was back in his favourite spot on the windowsill waiting for Rufus to appear in the tree. Sure enough after five minutes the big tabby cat arrived and sat on his favourite branch fixing Pickle with an insolent stare. *Right*, thought Pickle, *time to act.* He raced out into the garden and chased Rufus, right on his tail. Rufus, aware of Pickle right behind him, increased his speed and forgetting the big tree root tripped and fell. He tried to get up but couldn't, aware of a searing pain in his leg. Ouch! Pickle hissed but then realizing his arch rival was in trouble ran next door. Ruby was hanging out her washing.

"Well, hello Pickle my lad, you're all better then. Why, whatever is the matter, boy?" Pickle was miaowing loudly, looking hard at her and then running to the fence. She looked round the fence and saw Rufus in a heap on the grass. "Oh dear," she gasped, "I think we need to get you to the vet's."

Later that morning Pickle saw Roly and Ruby arrive home with Rufus in his cat carrier looking very sorry for himself. Patsy Purrkins, who was just returning from a walk with Lily, called out to them.

"Good morning, whatever has Rufus done to himself?"

"Well, he's done a Pickle and cut his paw," chuckled Roly. "He's going to be out of action for a couple of weeks I'm afraid."

"Oh dear, I am sorry to hear that, Roly, poor puss cat," said Patsy kindly.

*Good*, Pickle thought smugly as he headed to his basket for a nap. *Peace and quiet for a fortnight.* Now it was Rufus's turn to put up with a poorly paw.